SUN OF SUNS

TOR BOOKS BY KARL SCHROEDER

Lady of Mazes

Permanence

Ventus

Sun of Suns